D0270805

Other books by the author

The Idiot Family at Home

The Idiot Family on Holiday *to be published in 2013*

Perfectly Splendid Stories Collection

Archie Dingletrotter's Flying Caravan

Desmond's Dragon *to be published in 2013*

Perfectly Silly Stories Collection

Petronella Pumperknickel-Pinkstocking-Berck and Big Wart

The Phantom Sock-Snatcher *to be published in 2013*

From the Perfectly Splendid Stories Collection

Published by Stairmand Publishing 2012
Copyright © A J Stairmand 2012

A J Stairmand has asserted her moral right under the Copyright, Designs and Patents Act 1988 to be identified as the author of this work.

Illustration: Louisa Kewell

A CIP catalogue record for this book is available from the British Library.

ISBN 978-0-9569234-6-2

All rights reserved. No part of this publication may be reproduced, stored in a retrieval system or transmitted in any form or by any means (electronic, mechanical, photocopying, recording or otherwise) without the prior written permission of the publisher.

This book is sold subject to the condition that it shall not, by way of trade or otherwise, be lent, resold, hired out or otherwise circulated without the publisher's prior consent in any form of binding or cover other than that in which it is published and without a similar condition, including this condition, being imposed on the subsequent publisher.

Layout design by: Designsweet www.designsweet.co.uk

Printed by: Lavenham Press Limited
Arbons House, 47 Water Street, Lavenham CO10 9RN

Distributed by: York Publishing Services
64 Hallfield Road, Layerthorpe, York YO31 7ZQ

Acknowledgements

There are many people I would like to thank for all the support and help whilst writing and publishing this book. First of all, I would like to thank my ever-patient and truly wonderful editors, Sharon Burns, Kathy Norris and Michael, (my husband and biggest critic). Also, my sons James and Will, and my father, all of whom have been unwavering in their help, advice and expertise and, of course, their positive attitude.

In particular, I have to thank Kathy for her expertise, tireless commitment to the design of the layout, the finer details of the book, and the countless conversations over every single aspect.

I also have to give an enormous ***thank you*** to James Banfield for his support and advice which has been excellent, regarding the look and layout of this book and has been much appreciated. Adding to this, I have to thanks Leigh Hemmings for her time, ideas and enthusiasm for promoting my work this year, and always making me laugh!

I also need to give a ***MASSIVE thank you*** to Louisa Kewell for providing such wonderful and charming illustrations which really bring the story alive. Finding Louisa's drawings hidden away under a shelf in Waterstones Chelmsford, for a competition for one of my books, led me to ask her to illustrate this book... And what a great job she's done!

I need to also say a ***big thank you*** to Stoke by Nayland CEVC Primary School for allowing me to share the book with all the pupils, in its first draft. Their enthusiasm and enjoyment really encouraged me to develop the story, so I hope they enjoy the final result.

In fact, as I write this, I wish to thank Virginia Loveridge at Waterstones Chelmsford, and Dean Miguel at Waterstones Croydon, for unwavering support this year. Their enthusiasm and belief has been inspirational and so appreciated.

Most importantly, it's you the reader I wish to thank for reading my book. I really hope that you like it, enjoy it and have fun with the names and characters.

Chapter One

Archie Dingletrotter was nearly seven years old and had lived in more places than you and I could ever imagine. His life was like one long holiday because he was from a gypsy family, and moved from village to village every couple of months, which meant that Archie knew lots of people and lots of places.

Whenever he began at a new school, Archie often found he was the only child from a gypsy family, so he was very popular with children and teachers. Everyone always liked him as he was funny, kind, told entertaining stories of his family's adventures, and always tried hard at school. Even though he only stayed in a school two months or so at a time, Archie was very good at Maths, English, History, Art and, of course, Geography.

He really liked to work hard and do well, because he just loved going to new places and finding out about its history, and what the local people did. Wanting to learn came from his parents - his father Theobald and his mother Cressida, who loved explaining absolutely everything to Archie.

'Archie, it's so important for you to listen and learn all you can, so when you go to a new school, your teachers know that you have been working hard,' his mother always said, almost every night as he was finishing his diary for the day.

As he didn't really get homework, every night Cressida made him keep a diary. He had to read it out loud, and once a week he had to write a long story and use big, long words… to make it exciting.

Cressida worked hard and Archie couldn't quite make out why his mother was special, but he knew she was *'very special'*. She enjoyed making jam with all sorts of unusual and strange flavours, which, somehow, made people feel better. Her favourite was nettle and roseberry with nuts and plums, which cured any aches or pains. Another one was dandelion and daisy jam which made children behave well and do as they were told. But her favourite was leaf, grass and mint jelly, which she sold to rude, selfish and quite horrid people. Archie could never work out how villagers knew which jam to buy, but they always chose the one they needed, and often spent time talking to Cressida about strange and weird things.

Theobald also worked very hard. He

found work on local farms and helped on the land, or worked with blacksmiths making shoes for horses. He also helped people by building walls, tiling roofs, gardening or tidying up properties. Theobald loved the countryside and at the weekend would walk for miles with Archie, looking at the wildlife, the scenery, and getting to know the local people.

Archie could never quite believe his luck being a gypsy, as he was always getting ready to explore a new town or village.

Their caravan was painted in the colours of the rainbow. Inside there

WELCOME

were many scrap books brimming with information, leaflets, pictures and comments about villages the Dingletrotters had stayed in since Archie was a baby. Each one had a picture of the family on the front and main facts about each visit.

Chapter Two

One sunny day, Archie and his family arrived at a beautiful village in the countryside, which was surrounded by rolling hills, trees, bright flowers and animals playing contentedly in the fields.

'Cor Dad! This place looks great! Can we stay here for a bit and I could go to school in the village?' Archie beamed as he saw a babbling river winding through

the village, with flowers and wild grasses clustered on either side. People were busy going about their work. It all looked so happy and lovely. 'Go on Dad! We can go for loads of walks and I can make some more friends. I really like this place,' he said, tugging on his dad's shirt sleeve.

'I think this might be an interesting place,' commented Cressida, glancing at the village shops and people, as they drove through carefully, with their brightly coloured caravan.

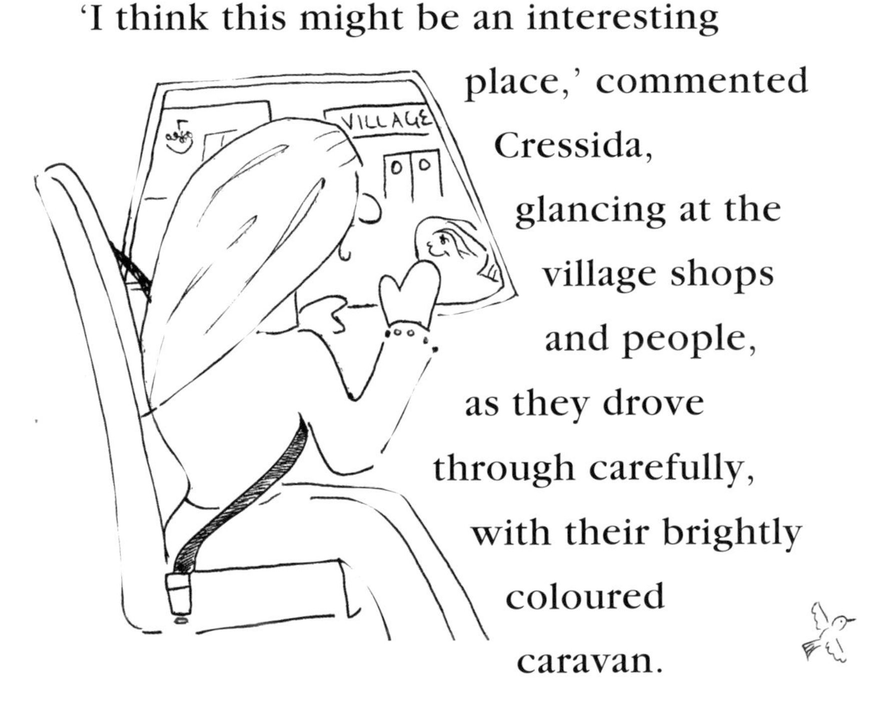

Stopping at the village green for an ice-cream, they sat perched on the edge of the small bridge. Archie trailed his tired feet in the water, whilst Cressida wafted her hand to stay cool. She knew Archie liked this place, and she had interesting feelings about it as well, and hoped that Theobald felt the same.

'I'll just have a look round to see if there's any work for me,' he said, finishing off his ice-cream before deciding where to explore. 'Don't worry Archie, it looks very promising, just let me have a chat and a look round.' Cressida and Archie smiled; they knew when he said this, things were looking good.

Sometime later, they saw Theobald coming down the road talking to a man in a checked jacket, laughing away as if they had known each other for years. He beckoned his family forward to meet the smiling stranger with white hair and a bushy beard. 'Meet Mr. Crumblelore, he has a farm just down the road and needs help with all his fences.

So come on, we have a field to stay in!' laughed Theobald, as he introduced the rest of the family to his new friend. Archie was thrilled, and liked Mr. Crumblelore, who was well-built, quite tall, and spoke with huge booming voice, which always seemed to be laughing.

'Well, Archie, I think you're going to like it here. The village school is great with lots of really, really, lovely children,

so you'll make loads of friends,' Mr. Crumblelore said shaking Archie's hand up and down. They all laughed and got the caravan ready to go to its new home at Cherry Tree Farm. Cressida knew she could make her special jams to sell in the village, and she secretly hoped, Theobald might decide to stay here for a long time.

It didn't take long for the Dingletrotters to become part of the farm. Archie helped out by getting up early to learn how to milk the cows, and clean out the stables with the farm helpers – who grew very

N
S

fond of him. Cressida spent the first few days collecting all the ingredients for making her jams and creating new recipes. Theobald just got on with building and repairing fences throughout the farm.

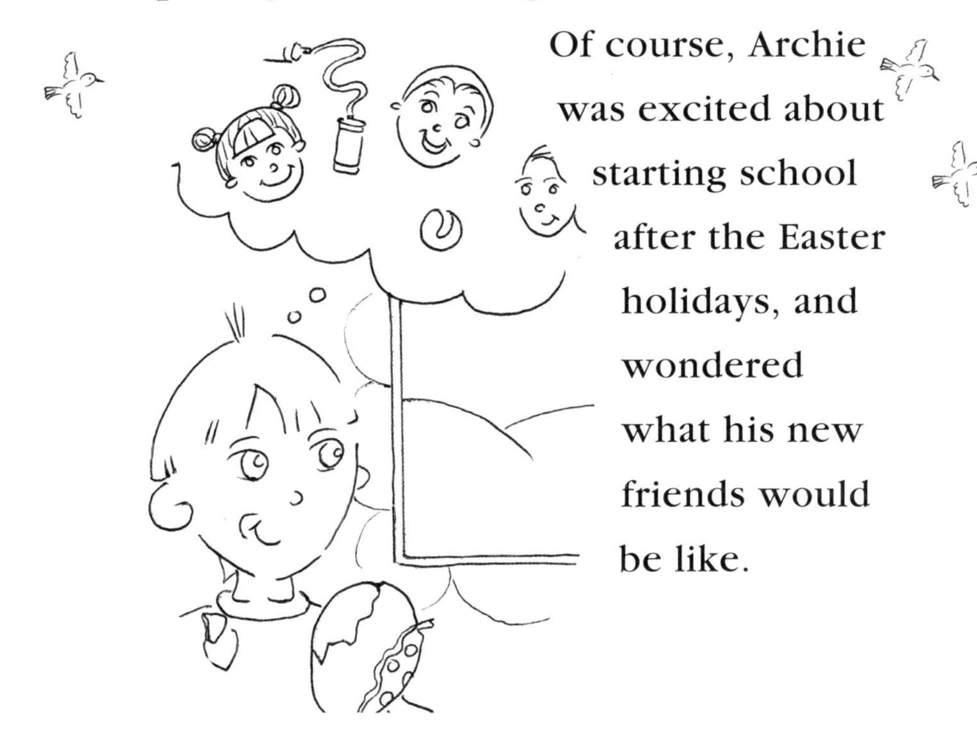

Of course, Archie was excited about starting school after the Easter holidays, and wondered what his new friends would be like.

Chapter Three

The school was near the village green by the river, and the sides of the bank were dotted with yellow and orange flowers. The old red building had high windows, gaily coloured pictures and mobiles hanging from the ceilings. There was a tall, green hedge surrounding the boundary at the front of the school, with a gate painted in bottle green.

Archie could hear the noise of children in the playground. They all sounded like they were having fun, he thought, as he walked towards the gates with Cressida.

'Shall I stay with you? I know you've done this many times Archie, but I think I'll just stay until you're settled in class and seem happy.' He nodded, and held her hand tightly as they walked into the entrance hall. A small woman, with black, curly hair and glasses, peeked from behind the partition and beckoned Cressida forward.

'Are you the new family staying at Cherry Tree Farm?' she asked, her nose twitching as Cressida nodded and smiled. 'Yes we are. And here is Archie,' she replied putting her hands on his shoulders so he could be seen.

'Fine. Now there's some paperwork needing to be filled in and then you have to wait to see the headteacher, who won't be long.' So, after filling in the forms they sat at the back of the hall watching the children laughing and singing in assembly. Everyone seemed so happy. Archie liked the look of all the displays, and loved the bright vibrant colours of the paintings and models.

'Hello Archie, I am Miss Mittletopple-Smulf, the head. Welcome to our tiny, but happy school!' She shook both Cressida and Archie's hands and showed them into her office. She was a very, very, tall lady with a small button nose, big green eyes, huge teeth (which reminded

Archie of a rabbit) and big, curly, ginger hair - and she seemed very nice. Cressida asked all the questions whilst Archie looked around the room, which was filled with pictures, flowers and odd objects, such as an oar from a rowing boat. At the end of their conversation they went to his class.

'This is your new teacher Archie, Mrs. Bagalotsnagalot, who will look after you.' The class was quiet, and the teacher showed him where to sit and then continued with the lesson. Everyone worked in silence, writing their news about the Easter holidays. Archie, used to writing lots in his diary, was finished before the bell for break, and had checked his work.

In the playground, Archie found he was the centre of attention and quickly made new friends – except for

three children in his own class who stared at him when he played football. After break, Mrs. Bagalotsnagalot asked Archie to read out his adventures in his last village, and his story was very funny and amusing.

He enjoyed his first day at school and told his parents how it went with his new friends.

'Everybody's friendly, except three in my class, two boys and a girl. I don't think they like me because I am a gypsy and don't have a big house,' said Archie as he ate a meal by the camp fire in the evening.

'Archie, I've never ever heard you say that before, about any of your new friends. People always love you, and want to be friends with you, because you are so funny, and good to people,' replied Cressida, a little worried and upset, as

she had always told him that his life and adventures were so exciting.

'Just be kind to everyone, and things will be fine Archie. Anyway, it's your birthday soon, so they'll all love your party in our field,' added Theobald, cooking sausages over the fire and looking into the flames.

'Not sure about that Dad, but we'll see.' With that, Archie went and got his diary to finish writing about his day at school.

Chapter Four

The next day there was lots of excitement as Bather Snellsbrook, one of the horrid three, had given out invitations to his party for Saturday at Castle Snodgrat, which was about four miles from the village. He handed Archie his invite saying, 'Well, I hope you don't feel left out at MY **HUGE** PARTY in

MY ENORMOUS CASTLE!' and marched away laughing, making Archie feel a little uncomfortable and sad. He loved his life and his parents, and he really loved his brightly coloured caravan.

The following day, which was Wednesday, Ermintrudel Flatterick handed out her invitations and gave one to Archie.

She sneered at him and said, 'I hope you don't find **MY** country house, Billowing Manor, too big, after **YOUR** little caravan.' Laughing, she went to join her friends. Archie looked down at the invitation and began to wish he hadn't started school here.

On Thursday, Meximore Troddlebut gave out his party invitations. Sniggering, he handed Archie a silver envelope. Inside was an invitation to his house on Klimpton Estate.

'My family owns all the land for MILES and MILES

and has done for hundreds and hundreds of years.

Don't worry if it's **too big** - I'll give you a map to get around!' and he roared with laughter as he went off to see his friends.

Archie was left on his own. Three invitations in three days. All from horrid children who wanted to show off and make him look and feel foolish about being a gypsy. At home Cressida said, 'Look Archie, you can enjoy the parties and have fun. It doesn't matter what other people have, and remember, nobody has been lucky enough to stay in such wonderful villages like you.' She smiled and gave him a hug, as she tucked him into his bunk to sleep.

'I'm sure you'll have a fantastic time, eat amazing cakes, and do lots of exciting activities at each one. Though I have to say Archie,' she whispered, 'with such dreadful names, it's not surprising they are not nice people. Anyway, it's your birthday soon and we'll have a special, very special party. You wait and see... everyone will want to be your best friend.' She said goodnight to Archie and finished potting her jams.

Chapter Five

As Archie approached the great big iron gates leading to Castle Snodgrat, he was amazed, because in the grounds there was the biggest, brightest fairground he had ever seen. All the children were having the most wonderful time, and they were eating the biggest ice-creams he had ever, ever, seen.

'Ah you came. Well you might as well join the others and play on **MY** fairground. Is this *my present*?'

questioned a greedy and bored Bather Snellsbrook, who had obviously been eating too much food. 'Is that it? It's **very** small. Oh! what can I expect...' and with that he grabbed the present and pointed to the rides for Archie to enjoy.

Archie didn't enjoy the party, not because the rides weren't fun, or because the food wasn't fantastic, but because Bather had been so rude to him and not enjoyed his present.

'Oh Archie, don't worry, your party will be soooooooo different', smiled his mother, as she heard about the castle, the huge walls, huge rooms and, of course, huge ice-creams.

On Sunday, the following day, Archie wrapped his small present and went off to Ermintrudel's party at Billowing Manor. From the gates he saw the biggest and brightest circus ever, with the tallest trapeze artists he had ever seen, and the cleverest acrobats he had ever watched.

'Well, I heard your presents were **small**, but…. is that really it?' a guzzling and burping Ermintrudel asked, in between enormous slurps of a fizzy drink,

which was running down her bursting dress. Archie just stared as she grabbed the present, tore the wrapping paper off, and ran to see her guzzling friends.

Again, Archie didn't enjoy the party, not because of the wonderful circus, or the wonderful food, but because Ermintrudel was so rude. This time he didn't even tell his parents. He said it was great and that he loved the circus.

The following Saturday, with his small present, Archie set off to Klimpton Estate where he was greeted by lots of action men at the gate. In the distance he could see a racing track, with all the children

from his class seated in specially designed racing cars having fun. There were also others eating the largest slices of cake he had ever seen. Ambling towards Archie, stuffing cake into his mouth, Meximore Troddlebut held out his hand for the present.

'Well, come on...give it now!! I've heard it's not much, but better than nothing. Give it **NOW**!!' The tiny, bony hands grabbed the present, threw it on the floor, and said,

'This isn't **big** enough for **me**! You might as well not have bothered!!

Well, come in and play!' With that he went off to race in a competition, leaving Archie to eat and play on all the amusements.

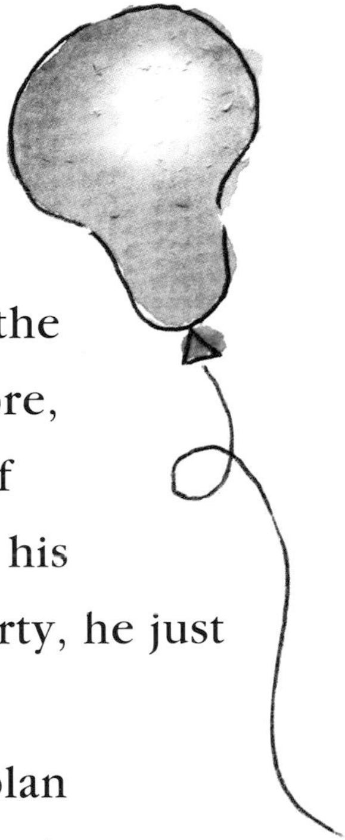

Oh, he really hated this party, well not the racing cars or activities, but the horrible rudeness of Meximore, who was quite the nastiest of the three. Of course, he told his mother it was an amazing party, he just didn't give any details.

'Well, we will have to plan for your birthday party and make it very special. I will make the biggest cake you could ever imagine, and your father will take the children to work with the animals…' chatted his mother, only to be interrupted by a huge

‘NNNNNNNNNNNNNNNOOOOOOOOOOOOOOOO!!!!!!

Everyone will laugh and make fun of me for not having a big castle, manor or lots of land.

I don't want a party with horrid people saying cruel and nasty things....' And Archie began to cry, and cry, and cry, and in between the tears, he told Cressida about all the parties.

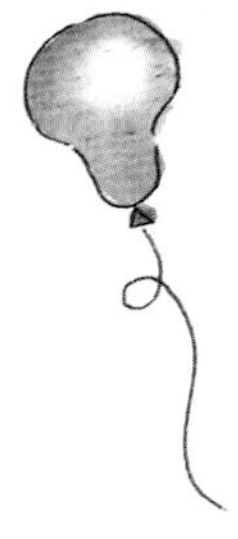

Chapter Six

Cressida made the cake, and it was the biggest, and the most colourful one she had ever done.

It was fantastic and looked like a caravan with candles.

'There!! Isn't this the most wonderful cake ever?' smiled his mother as she got all the food ready for Archie's party in the afternoon. He nodded, but didn't

dare tell her that at the parties of three horrid children, everyone had to climb a ladder to get their slice, as the cakes were so huge. He wondered what everyone would make of his caravan – up to now all his friends had loved it, but today, he wasn't sure.

Cressida smiled and laughed, 'What a special, unusual day this is going to be with your friends. Now, forget about those ones in the castle, they might have a good time too!' She laughed as she decorated the caravan in balloons and bows.

As the party began, his new friends started running into the field with their presents, excited to see Archie's colourful caravan. They were amazed to find it so beautiful.

Immediately, they all wanted to stay and camp in the field, and have their food on an open fire. Archie was pleased; he had made some lovely new friends, though deep down he was still dreading the arrival of Meximore, Bather and Ermintrudel. He knew they wouldn't enjoy the party, and worse, might spoil it for the others. Just as he thought this, there in the distance, he saw them all arriving in big, shiny cars.

As they walked towards the caravan, they stuck their noses in the air, taking care not to get dirt on their shoes.

'Are *we* expected to eat *here*?' asked Ermintrudel, patting down her pink silk dress with her new white gloves.

'Well, we'll stay just a little bit and have

some of '*this*' food', Meximore whispered to the other two, sneering as he looked at the children playing games in the field.

Archie greeted them and thanked them for their gifts - oh they were **big** and wrapped in bright glistening paper.

'Now come on all of you! Over here and we'll have some cake inside the caravan! Come on!' The children scrambled to take off their shoes, and squeezed onto the seats ready for a slice of Cressida's amazing cake. The sponge was pink, green, blue, red, yellow and purple - and everyone loved it, except the three spoilt guests, who were determined to be difficult.

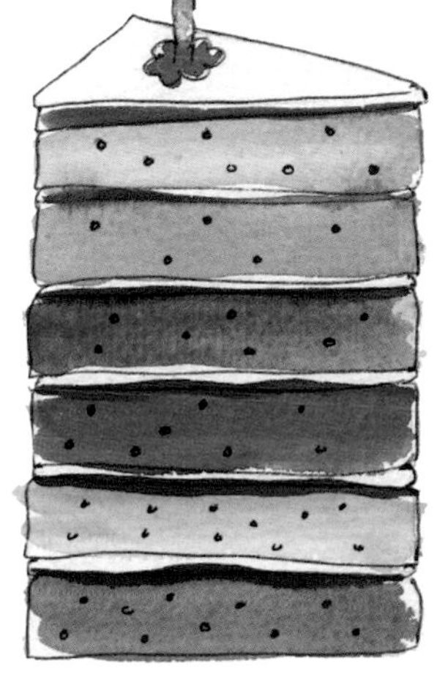

'I don't eat anything red!' said Bather.

'I don't eat in squashed seats. I always have my own

seat!' added Meximore, refusing the cake with a flick of his hand.

'I only eat in the best places! This is sooo boring!' snarled Ermintrudel, refusing the cake.

'Well,' said Cressida slowly, 'well, you three had better go outside and sit on the seats. You need to wait for your parents to collect you as you are bored.

So out you go!'

They sat on the seats outside looking bored and glum, whilst they waited for their parents to collect them.

Suddenly, inside the caravan there was a rumbling sound. 'I'll just check things are alright' smiled Cressida as she disappeared outside. The caravan started rocking from side to side, and making gurgling noises. The children sat still and waited for Cressida to come back.

She didn't.

Archie was getting a little bit worried. He didn't know what was happening.......

WHOOOSH!

The caravan suddenly hovered, growled like an engine, then whizzed high into the sky, rocking as it gained height and speed. Archie sat frozen, not with fear, but with joy and happiness.

The children laughed and clapped, as the caravan twisted and twirled through the air, making shapes in the clouds. It zoomed over the village, passing the castle, manor house and estate, which all looked so small from the sky. The caravan spun through the air, spinning and turning, swooping through the clouds, and diving to skim just over the trees in the local woods.

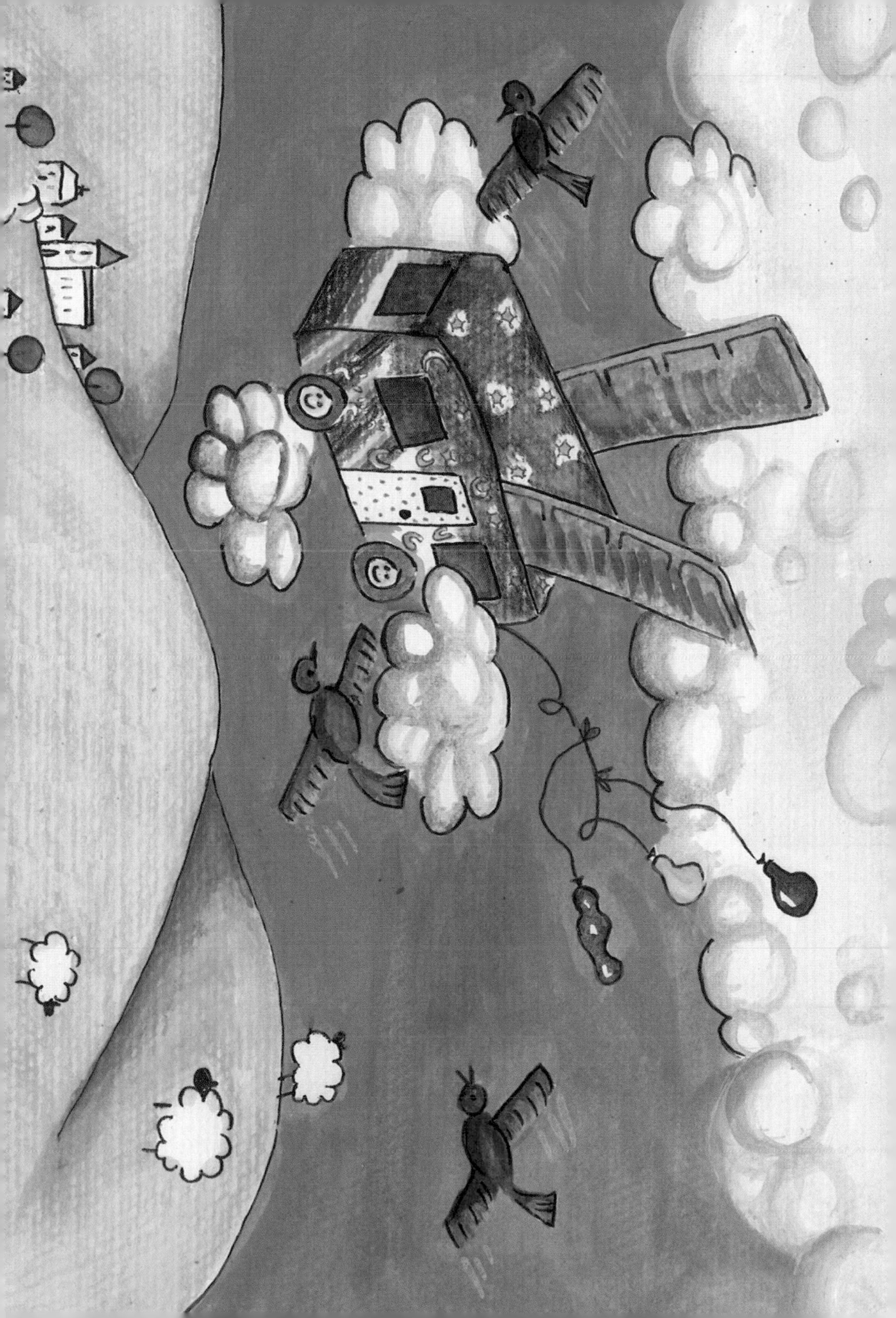

As if that wasn't enough, as they flew through the sky, delighted, shocked and amazed, something else wonderful started to happen. The caravan began singing and chiming

'**Wow!**' exclaimed Archie, 'this is the best party in the whole world! Fancy! Having 'my own' flying caravan, on **my** birthday. How wonderful!!' he beamed to his friends. They were all singing along to the song, and peering out of the windows, thrilled at everything they saw.

As Archie looked down to the field where his three horrible guests were, he saw them jumping up and down, stamping their feet and crying. He quietly smiled.

Of course, once the caravan landed safely back in the field, it was surrounded by all the villagers, who clapped and

HAPPY BIRTHDAY

shouted for joy at such a wonderful sight.

Archie was famous. Actually, his caravan was famous too!

And from that moment on, nobody was bothered about having a party in a castle, or a manor house, or a country estate. Everybody wanted to fly in Archie's flying caravan... except for his three horrid guests, who sat and sulked, and continued to stamp their feet.

Archie was the happiest boy in the world, but couldn't understand how his caravan was magic and could fly.

'I didn't know our caravan was magic. How did that happen?' he asked his parents one night as they ate by the fireside.

Cressida just smiled and winked at Theobald.

Anne Stairmand was born in North Yorkshire, living much of her life in villages near the Cleveland Hills. After graduating, she worked in education, teaching in both primary and secondary schools in the south east, working in the advisory service and as part of a leadership team.

Dividing her time, she now writes books for children and adults, and has her own business as a bespoke jeweller, with her own hallmark and stamp, specialising in silver, pearls and commissions. She is married with a grown-up family and lives on the Suffolk Essex border.

Author visits and workshops in schools

Become an author for a day!

Anne is available for author visits to schools which are stimulating. Using her expertise in literacy and education she supplies a package that is not only challenging and innovative, but can help improve writing back in the classroom.

Resources linked to the curriculum are made to cater for each class/group, so afterwards can be used as a tool to support literacy at KS1, KS2 and KS3.

Fun days with lots of excitement which also develop writing and literacy skills.

A variety of packages available to suit needs, enjoyment and, of course, budget.

Contact:
Email: annestairmandj@hotmail.co.uk
www.annestairmand.co.uk